For Ben and Ollie

OXFORD
UNIVERSITY PRESS

Great Clarendon Street, Oxford OX2 6DP

Oxford University Press is a department of the University of Oxford.
It furthers the University's objective of excellence in research, scholarship,
and education by publishing worldwide in Oxford New York Auckland
Cape Town Dar es Salaam Hong Kong Karachi Kuala Lumpur Madrid
Melbourne Mexico City Nairobi New Delhi Shanghai Taipei Toronto

With offices in Argentina Austria Brazil Chile Czech Republic France
Greece Guatemala Hungary Italy Japan Poland Portugal Singapore South
Korea Switzerland Thailand Turkey Ukraine Vietnam

Oxford is a registered trade mark of Oxford University Press
in the UK and in certain other countries

Text and illustrations © Richard Byrne 2018

The moral rights of the author/illustrator have been asserted Database right
Oxford University Press (maker)

First published in 2018

ISBN: 978-0-19-274976-5 (hardback)
ISBN: 978-0-19-274977-2 (paperback)

10 9 8 7 6 5 4 3 2 1

Printed in China

Paper used in the production of this book is a natural, recyclable product made
from wood grown in sustainable forests. The manufacturing process conforms to
the environmental regulations of the country of origin.

Visit www.richardbyrne.co.uk

THE CASE OF THE RED-BOTTOMED ROBBER!

Richard BYRNE

OXFORD
UNIVERSITY PRESS

The young chalks were having a
fabulous time at the chalkboard
when Mrs Red called them in for . . .

When the chalks came back from lunch
they got a real shock.

The chalks started a new drawing but this time
Mrs Red also drew a big red fence.

'That should keep the flowers safe while we go in for a story,' she said.

But it didn't.
The flowers had disappeared AGAIN!

And this time the fence had gone, too!

Sergeant Blue arrived
to investigate . . .

So he rounded up some suspicious-looking characters.

'Too thin . . .

Too small . . .

GLUE

Too pointy . . .

Case closed!

But before Sergeant Blue could
put the culprit in prison . . .

...the robber fled in a cloud of dust.

And although the chalks gave chase....

...the robber was too fast for them.

The chalks had no idea how they were
going to catch the elusive robber . . .

...but fortunately
Sergeant Blue had a plan.

The robber was sure he had given the chalks the slip.
Then he stumbled across a very tempting new drawing.

RAINBOW-RUBBING HERE I COME!

The chalks suddenly leapt out
from their hiding places.

ROBBER!
CAUGHT YOU!

The chalkboard duster felt wrongly accused.

I'm innocent!
I'm not a robber, I'm a DUSTER!
You draw stuff and I rub it out,
then you can draw more stuff!

The chalks felt very guilty. They had made a terrible mistake.

Sergeant Blue knew how to put things right. They should all chase the duster again . . .

... but this time
just for fun!